"Susan Hunt leads children through Psalm 23, one verse at a time, looking in detail at a shepherd's care through the eyes of his sheep. *Sammy and His Shepherd* explains important doctrines in simple and concise terms *and* points out how those doctrines about our Shepherd should impact the everyday lives of His sheep. This is a visually attractive book that sets forth the beauty of our Lord."

—**Starr Meade**
Author, *Keeping Holiday* and *Training Hearts, Teaching Minds*

"*Sammy and His Shepherd* is a delightful book for children. Written as an imaginative story narrated by a young lamb, this book does a skillful exposition of Psalm 23. It even includes some great talking points for each chapter. Susan Hunt's skills as a writer and rich theological insights are beautifully crafted into this story. Here is a book children will grow into and never outgrow."

—**Tedd Tripp**
Pastor, conference speaker, and author, *Shepherding a Child's Heart*

"I gave Susan Hunt's latest book the real test: I began reading it out loud to my rambunctious five-year-old. He was immediately charmed by her storytelling ability and would not let me stop. *Sammy and His Shepherd* combines rich, theologically informed understanding with sanctified creativity to reveal the green pastures of God's sovereign grace in all its loveliness."

—**Douglas Bond**
Author, Crown & Covenant series and Faith & Freedom trilogy

"In this lovely book on the best-loved psalm, Susan Hunt engages the attention in a delightful way. I would encourage families to use this book and take advantage of the clear teaching, which points to the Good Shepherd who loves children and demonstrated that love so gloriously at Calvary."

—**Carine Mackenzie**
Author, Bible Time series and Bible Wise series

SAMMY AND HIS SHEPHERD

•••••••••••••••••••••

SEEING JESUS IN PSALM 23

Written by Susan Hunt

Illustrated by Cory Godbey

 Reformation Trust   A DIVISION OF LIGONIER MINISTRIES, ORLANDO, FL

Sammy and His Shepherd: Seeing Jesus in Psalm 23

Text: © 2008 by Susan Hunt
Illustrations: © 2008 by Cory Godbey

Published by Reformation Trust Publishing
a division of Ligonier Ministries
421 Ligonier Court, Sanford, FL 32771
Ligonier.org   ReformationTrust.com

Printed in Reynosa, Tamaulipas, Mexico
RR Donnelley and Sons
November 2013
First edition, fifth printing

Creative direction: Geoff Stevens
Cover and interior design: Tobias' Outerwear for Books

Unless otherwise indicated, all Scripture quotations are from *The Holy Bible, English
Standard Version*, copyright © 2001 by Crossway Bibles, a division of Good News
Publishers. Used by permission. All rights reserved.

Library of Congress Cataloging-in-Publication Data
Hunt, Susan, 1940-
        Sammy and his shepherd / by Susan Hunt ; illustrations by Cory Godbey.
                p. cm.
"Seeing Jesus in Psalm 23."
Summary: Sammy the sheep explains to a neighboring sheep how his loving
shepherd takes care of him and keeps him safe. Includes the text of Psalm 23 and
suggested discussion questions.
ISBN 978-1-56769-109-2
[1. Sheep--Fiction. 2. Christian life--Fiction. 3. Allegories. 4. Bible. O.T. Psalm XXIII.]
I. Godbey, Cory, ill. II. Title.
PZ7.H916534Sam 2008
[Fic]--dc22

                                                        2008027004

PREFACE

Dear lovers of children:

Thank you for loving children enough to read to them. The coziness of sitting together with a good book and the familiarity of hearing your voice read and reread a favorite story create treasured memories. When the book points a child to the Savior, the experience is eternally significant.

Psalm 23 is a celebration of the comprehensiveness of salvation by grace. Helping a child memorize this beloved psalm bestows a treasure that cannot be taken away. Read it each time you read the story and soon the child will join in. Talking about the story and praying together will expand his or her understanding. (Discussion questions and activities for each chapter can be found beginning on page 44.)

My husband and I have twelve grandchildren. Sometimes I ponder the question: If I could give them only one portion of Scripture, what would it be? I could never select just one, but Psalm 23 is surely on the short list. My prayer is that this little book will help children—and those who read to them—to delight in the knowledge that Jesus is the Good Shepherd, that we are saved and kept by grace, and that we are privileged to live as a part of the flock of God's people.

For the glory of the Shepherd who became the Lamb who is the King.

—Susan Hunt
Marietta, Georgia
July 2008

PSALM 23

The LORD is my shepherd; I shall not want.
He makes me lie down in green pastures.
He leads me beside still waters.
He restores my soul.
He leads me in paths of righteousness
for his name's sake.
Even though I walk through the valley
of the shadow of death,
I will fear no evil, for you are with me;
your rod and your staff, they comfort me.
You prepare a table before me
in the presence of my enemies;
you anoint my head with oil;
my cup overflows.
Surely goodness and mercy shall follow me
all the days of my life,
and I shall dwell in the house of the LORD forever.

THE LORD IS MY SHEPHERD; I SHALL NOT WANT

I'm such a happy sheep," Sammy thought as he grazed contentedly in the lush pasture.

He looked up and noticed a sheep in the next pasture looking longingly through the fence. He also noticed that the other pasture was not as nice as his.

"I never noticed how many rocks and how little grass are in that pasture," he thought.

Sammy ambled toward the fence. "Hi," he called to the other sheep. "What's your name?"

"I don't have a name," the sheep said.

Sammy tried not to appear shocked, but he couldn't imagine a sheep not having a name. Then he noticed that the sheep was very skinny and that flies were buzzing around her head.

The little sheep asked, "Do you have a name?"

"My name is Samuel, but everyone calls me Sammy."

"Where did you get your name?"

"My shepherd named me soon after he bought me. He names all of his sheep."

"Why does he do that?" the sheep asked as she shook her head to try to make the flies go away.

"Well, I guess because he loves each one of us and he knows us by name. Samuel means 'heard by God.' I was wounded and sick when my shepherd bought me, and he prayed for me. He named me Samuel so that I would always remember that God heard his prayer."

"You sure seem happy," the little sheep said.

"Of course I'm happy. I have the best shepherd in the whole world. I know that I will never want for anything."

"How can you know that?"

"Because my shepherd loves me and he always takes care of me," Sammy answered.

"I don't understand," the little sheep said. "Look at this pasture. There's never enough grass to eat. I'm always hungry. And our water isn't very good either."

"I'm sorry you're hungry," Sammy replied. "I always have enough food and water because my shepherd provides everything I need."

"Do you mean that you never have to walk through scary valleys or climb high hills to get to different pastures?"

"Oh, no, I don't mean that I never have to go to hard places. But my shepherd is always with me and he helps me go through those hard places."

"But what about the enemies waiting to attack you?" the little sheep asked.

"My shepherd always guards me, no matter how dangerous it is. He would even lay down his life to protect me."

"I wish I had a shepherd I could trust," the little sheep moaned.

Talking to the little sheep made Sammy grateful for his shepherd. He also felt sad for the scrawny sheep and wanted to show kindness to her, but he didn't know what to do. Then he had an idea.

"Can we be friends?" Sammy asked. He noticed that the little sheep's eyes brightened, so he continued, "Since you don't have a name, I'm going to call you 'My Friend.'"

The little sheep seemed to stand a bit taller and she certainly looked happier. "I like that," she said. "I'll see you tomorrow."

"Same time, same fence," Sammy laughed.

"TALK ABOUT IT."
CHAPTER 1 • PAGE 44

HE MAKES ME LIE DOWN IN GREEN PASTURES

Hi, My Friend," Sammy called as he waddled to the fence.

"Hi, Sammy. What have you been doing?"

"Well," Sammy yawned, "I just got up. I've been snoozing on the other side of the pasture. It was soooo restful."

My Friend looked puzzled. "How can you lie down and rest with so many distractions?"

"I don't have any distractions," Sammy replied.

"But aren't you afraid that something terrible will happen to you?"

"No," Sammy answered.

"What about the bigger sheep, or the flies and insects . . . and aren't you just too hungry to lie down and rest?" My Friend quizzed.

Sammy was a bit bewildered. "No, My Friend. I don't worry about any of those things. My shepherd takes care of everything so that I can lie down and rest."

"I wish I belonged to your shepherd," My Friend said as a bigger sheep butted her with his head and pushed her away.

Once again Sammy felt sad for the little sheep. He was so troubled that he didn't notice Grandma mosey up beside him. She wasn't really his grandmother, but all the sheep called her that because she was the oldest sheep in the flock. Sammy was startled when he heard Grandma's

kind old voice.

"Sammy," she said, "do you understand why your friend can't lie down and rest?"

"No, ma'am."

"Let me tell you about sheep," Grandma said. "We cannot lie down and rest unless four things are done for us."

"Really? What are those four things?"

"First," Grandma said, "we must not be afraid. We are easily frightened because we're helpless. Think about it, Sammy. We have no way to defend ourselves. One dog or coyote can terrify a whole flock of sheep. Without a shepherd to protect us, we are too afraid to lie down."

"I never thought about that, but you're right, Grandma. What's the second thing we need?"

"There must not be any bickering with other sheep in the flock. We can be very cruel to each other. Bigger, aggressive sheep bully weaker sheep. Bossy sheep push the others away from the best grazing places. When we're squabbling, we can't lie down and rest. But our shepherd stops our silly fights. Then we can rest."

"You're right again, Grandma," Sammy laughed. "What's the third thing we need?"

"We must be peaceful. This means we must be free from flies and parasites swarming around our heads and up our noses. Those pesky bugs drive us crazy. I've seen sheep shake their heads and stamp their hoofs trying to get rid of them. I seem to remember that you had a problem with nose flies once."

"Yep. I'll never forget that," Sammy exclaimed.

"A good shepherd applies special oil to his sheep. This oil keeps the bugs away. Then we are peaceful and we can lie down and rest."

"Grandma, hanging out with you makes me a wiser sheep. Now tell me the fourth thing we need."

"You do know how to make an old sheep feel special," Grandma chuckled. "The fourth thing we need is food. We cannot lie down if we're hungry. A good shepherd clears the pasture of rocks, prepares the soil, and plants grain so that his sheep will have plenty to eat. Look at your friend's rocky pasture. There's not much grass there. Now look at our beautiful green pasture. Sammy, why do you think there is such a difference?"

"Because we belong to a good shepherd who prepares green pastures for us. I'm glad I belong to our shepherd."

Grandma nodded in agreement. "I've belonged to him for a very long time, Sammy, and every day I am more thankful that he makes me lie down in green pastures."

"TALK ABOUT IT."
CHAPTER 2 · PAGE 45

CHAPTER THREE

HE LEADS ME BESIDE STILL WATERS

The first glimmers of light peeked through the boards of the sheepfold. "It's almost time," Sammy thought. He knew his shepherd would be there soon because a good shepherd takes his sheep to the pasture while dew is still on the grass. Dew is a source of water for sheep, but in order for them to get it, they have to get to the pasture early.

"Here he is," Sammy called to the other sheep. The shepherd led them out, and soon they were munching the clean, moist grass.

Early morning was Sammy's favorite time of the day. The air was crisp, the grass was yummy, and everything was still as the night softly melted into day. Sammy called it his quiet time. He liked to use the time to think about all of his blessings. This day, Sammy thought about how much he loved the other sheep.

He looked around and spotted old Gus. "I know Gus is grumpy sometimes, but I do love him," Sammy thought.

He saw Prissy. "She drives us all crazy with her persnicketiness," he grinned. "But every flock needs a prissy sheep."

Then he saw Grandma. "She's so old and feeble," Sammy thought. "We all have to help her, but she's so wise. We're all better and stronger because she's part of our flock."

Soon he had thought of something he loved about every sheep in the flock. "I wonder why I love them so much, especially since we are all so

different?" He pondered this question for a while, then he exclaimed, "I know why we all love each other—it's because we belong to the same shepherd and he loves every one of us." Sammy smiled as he thought about his kind shepherd, who always provided all that the sheep needed, including fresh water.

Suddenly Sammy noticed that the pasture on the other side of the fence was empty. "Oh, no, the dew is almost gone and My Friend and her flock aren't here yet," he worried.

Sammy didn't see My Friend at the fence until later that morning. She looked even thinner and weaker, and Sammy knew that it was because she had not had enough food and water.

"Hi, My Friend," Sammy said, trying to sound cheerful. "Where were you this morning? There was a heavy dew on the ground."

"I was in the sheep pen. My shepherd didn't let us out until all the dew was gone."

"I'm sorry," Sammy sympathized. "Does he take you to a quiet stream where you can get water?"

"The place he takes us has dirty water that is full of parasites. Sometimes I get sick drinking it," My Friend replied.

Sammy felt sorry for My Friend, but hearing these things made him even more grateful for his good shepherd. He was thankful that his shepherd always provided good water for his flock, both by making sure they got to the pasture while the dew was still on the grass and by leading them to quiet streams.

"TALK ABOUT IT."
CHAPTER 3 · PAGE 47

CHAPTER FOUR

HE RESTORES MY SOUL

···

I wonder where she is," Sammy worried.

He watched the fence all day, hoping to see My Friend. Finally he thought, "Maybe she's over the hill, and if I go to the fence she'll see me and come visit."

When Sammy got to the fence, he was horrified. He could see My Friend in the distance, and she was cast down. She was lying on her back and her feet were in the air, flailing frantically. Sammy knew that her blood would stop circulating and she would die if her shepherd did not come soon.

Sammy grew hysterical. "My Friend is helpless," he cried. "She can't roll over and get back on her feet." He butted his head against the fence. "Baa, baa."

His shepherd, who was always close by, saw Sammy's frenzy and ran to him. "Sammy, Sammy, it's all right," he said softly. Usually the shepherd's presence calmed Sammy, but not this time. He continued to butt his head against the fence.

The shepherd looked up and saw My Friend. In a flash, he jumped over the fence and ran to the helpless sheep. He gently lifted My Friend, turned her over, and stood her up on her feet. Then he rubbed her legs so the blood would circulate. Finally, My Friend took a few wobbly steps.

As Sammy watched his good shepherd, he remembered the first time he had become cast down. He had been terrified, but his shepherd had helped him.

Afterward, the shepherd had spoken to him gently, explaining what had happened. "Sometimes a sheep like you can roll over on his back," the shepherd said. "When that happens, we say the sheep is cast down. A cast-down sheep cannot turn himself back over. If someone doesn't help the sheep, he will die. He needs someone to restore him to a right position."

Sammy gave the shepherd a quizzical look.

The shepherd smiled. "You have to be careful, Sammy. A sheep can become cast down in many ways. If he lies in a soft, squishy spot, his round little body will topple over on his back. Or sometimes a sheep gets clumps of mud or bits of bushes tangled in his fleece, and he becomes so heavy that he rolls over.

"So be careful, Sammy. But remember, if you do become cast down, I will be there to help you."

Sammy was thankful that his shepherd always came and restored him to a right position when he became cast down. "My shepherd never leaves me. He always watches over me. He always comes and helps me," Sammy thought gratefully.

"TALK ABOUT IT."
CHAPTER 4 • PAGE 48

HE LEADS ME IN PATHS OF RIGHTEOUSNESS FOR HIS NAME'S SAKE

My Friend stood at the fence and watched wistfully as the good shepherd began to guide his sheep to another pasture.

The shepherd knew that silly sheep will eat in the same spot even when all the grass is gone and there is nothing left but roots, so he was ready to move his sheep to another pasture where there was fresh grass.

"My shepherd never takes us to a different pasture, and this pasture has become nothing but hard ground," My Friend thought.

Suddenly she made a decision. Hoping no one would notice, she ducked her head under the fence and began trying to wriggle through to the other side. But the space between the bottom board of the fence and the ground was smaller than My Friend had thought. Soon she was stuck. The more she squirmed, the more frantic she became. She could hardly breathe. She bleated pitifully.

My Friend's shepherd was sleeping under a tree, but the commotion woke him. He was very irritated as he ambled toward her. Sammy's shepherd also saw My Friend's predicament, but he ran to the fence. Sammy ran over when he realized that it was My Friend struggling under the fence.

My Friend's shepherd yelled and lifted his rod to strike her, but Sammy's shepherd arrived just in the nick of time. "Wait! Don't hurt her. I'll get her out," he said.

"She's just a worthless sheep," her shepherd sneered. "And now she's trying to run away. She's not worth saving."

The good shepherd reached down and gently dug some dirt from under My Friend. Sammy tried to reassure her. "It's OK," he said. "My shepherd will get you out."

Finally the shepherd freed My Friend from the fence. He picked her up and held her tenderly in his arms. "I will buy her from you," he said to the other shepherd.

"Why do you want to buy her? She's so sickly she'll probably die."

The good shepherd smiled. "Maybe so, but I love her and I want her to be one of my sheep."

He paid the man and began to walk across the pasture holding the dirty, sickly sheep. Sammy skipped along beside the shepherd, bursting with happiness.

As he walked, the shepherd whispered to My Friend. "Now you belong to me," he said. "The only way you could become part of my flock was for me to redeem you—to buy you. But now you are mine. No one can ever take you away from me. I will never leave you, and I will always lead you on good paths.

"Now," he grinned, "what shall I name you?"

My Friend tingled with excitement as she waited. She could see the love in her shepherd's eyes as he thought about her name. "Of course!" he exclaimed. "I will name you Precious, because you are precious to me."

Her eyes welled with happy tears. "Precious . . . my name is Precious," she thought. "I am precious to my shepherd." For the first time in her life, she felt safe and loved. She was full of gratitude. In her heart she said: "Now I belong to a good shepherd. I shall not want for anything. He will make me lie down in green pastures. He will lead me beside still waters. He will restore me when I am cast down. He will lead me in good paths."

"TALK ABOUT IT."

CHAPTER 5 • PAGE 49

EVEN THOUGH I WALK THROUGH THE VALLEY OF THE SHADOW OF DEATH, I WILL FEAR No EVIL, FoR YoU ARE WITH ME

The first thing Precious thought every morning and the last thing she thought every night was, "I belong to the good shepherd. I am precious to him."

One day, she listened eagerly as her shepherd explained, "Tomorrow we begin our trip to the high places."

Precious looked at Sammy. "Where are the high places? Why are we going there?" she asked.

Sammy and Precious had become even closer friends since the shepherd had redeemed her. Sammy took special delight in helping Precious learn the ways of her new flock.

"The high places are wonderful," Sammy replied. "It's almost summer. It will be hot and dry here, so there won't be much grass, but on the mountains there will be beautiful green grass and fresh cool streams."

"But I'm afraid to climb up the high mountains," Precious exclaimed.

"You don't have to be afraid. Our shepherd will be with us. But there is something very important that you must remember."

"What? Tell me quickly."

Sammy smiled. "Our shepherd is always before us, leading the way. When it is dark and you can't see him, just listen for his voice."

"Do you think I'll recognize his voice?" Precious asked.

"Oh, yes. You'll know his voice because you belong to him. He will guide us through valleys and up to the places he has prepared for us."

The next day, the flock started on the journey. They slowly climbed uphill, then they came to a valley. The verdant grass was yummy, but the mountains and cliffs on all sides made the valley seem dark and scary.

Precious was still weak and soon grew tired. She could not keep up with the other sheep and became very afraid. Soon she began to cry. "What if they leave me and I get lost?" she thought.

Then she saw her shepherd coming back for her. She heard his strong and gentle voice say: "My little Precious, are you tired and afraid? Let me carry you for a while." He picked her up and cradled her gently in his strong arms.

Precious relaxed. As the shepherd carried her along, she thought: "Now I'm not afraid. I will fear no evil in this scary valley because my shepherd is with me."

"TALK ABOUT IT."
CHAPTER 6 • PAGE 50

CHAPTER SEVEN

YOUR ROD AND YOUR STAFF, THEY COMFORT ME

As the flock continued its climb to the high places, Precious began to worry again. Troubled thoughts were running around wildly in her head. She was quite startled when Sammy waddled up alongside her and said, "Good morning, Precious."

Precious was so flustered that her words tumbled out on top of each other. "Is it good? Maybe I should never have come. Do I really belong here? What if the other sheep don't like me? Will I like the high places? What if I get lost? What if something attacks me? What if I fall over a cliff?"

"Precious, calm down. Look at our shepherd."

They both looked ahead and saw their shepherd standing on a rock, watching over his sheep.

"Can you see what he is holding?" Sammy asked.

Precious was perturbed that Sammy asked her such a simple question when she had such a serious problem. "He's holding his shepherd equipment—his rod and his staff," she answered.

"That's right," Sammy said. "When I become afraid or agitated, I remember that our shepherd always has his rod and his staff."

Precious looked at Sammy. "Well, I don't mean to be rude," she said, "but I really don't know why that should comfort me."

"Well, you see, it's like this. On my first journey to the high places, I

was pretty stubborn. I decided to wander off and see the sights. I had taken only a few steps when our shepherd's rod whizzed by me. I scurried back to the flock as fast as my short legs would carry me. Later I realized that going my own way will get me in trouble, and that our good shepherd will discipline me when I try to wander away."

'Well," Precious sighed, "I don't plan to stray on purpose, but I guess it is a comfort to know that if I'm careless and wander off our shepherd will use his rod to warn me."

"And that's not all," Sammy exclaimed. "Another time I was grazing and the rod whooshed by me. I looked up and saw a wolf dart away. I knew that the shepherd had protected me from an attack."

Precious cocked her head. "Now, that's comforting," she said.

"There's more," Sammy said. "One day I was so greedy that I kept eating right to the edge of a cliff and suddenly found myself in a free fall over the side."

"Oh, Sammy. What happened?" Precious asked.

"I landed on a ledge. I was so frightened that I couldn't make a sound. That afternoon, when the shepherd counted his sheep, he realized I was missing. He left all the others and searched until he found me. Then he reached his long staff down, scooped me up with the crook, and rescued me."

"Ahhh," Precious smiled. Her eyes sparkled. "Now I feel peaceful. His rod and his staff comfort me, too."

"TALK ABOUT IT."
CHAPTER 7 · PAGE 51

You PREPARE A TABLE BEFoRE ME IN THE PRESENCE oF My ENEMIES

W e're almost there," Sammy panted.

"I hope so," Precious groaned. "I have never been so high in the mountains. Are you sure this is a good place for us to spend the summer? I'm not sure I'm going to like being on a hill all the time. What if I start rolling down and can't stop?"

Sammy sighed. He knew he had to be patient with Precious, but sometimes he wondered whether she would ever learn to trust their shepherd. Then he remembered his first trip to the high places and how others had taught and encouraged him, so he explained: "You don't need to worry, Precious. We're going to a tableland."

"What's a tableland?"

"It's level ground, and it's wonderful because our shepherd has prepared it for us."

"When did he prepare it?" Precious asked.

Sammy smiled as he thought about his shepherd. "He made this journey before he brought us here. He came ahead and made it ready for us."

"What did he have to do to get it ready?"

Sometimes it seemed that Precious had a zillion questions, but Sammy enjoyed answering them because he loved to tell her about their shepherd. "He got rid of harmful enemies."

"What?" Precious gasped. "You mean there are enemies on the tableland?"

"Well," Sammy said, "there were poisonous flowers and weeds growing among the grass. We can't tell the difference between what's good and what will kill us, but our shepherd knows. He came and cleared the ground of all the things that can harm us. There's a spring with delicious fresh water, but it gets dirty during the winter. Our shepherd cleaned out the leaves and dirt so that we can drink from it. He prepared the tableland for us."

"So there are no more enemies?" Precious asked.

"There will always be some enemies. Sometimes wolves creep up behind rocks and watch us, but we don't have to be afraid. We can relax and enjoy this tableland even when enemies are watching us because our shepherd is watching them. He will protect us."

Precious thought about this for a while and then said: "Our shepherd thinks of everything. He even gave me a friend like you to answer my questions."

"TALK ABOUT IT."
CHAPTER 8 • PAGE 53

YOU ANOINT MY HEAD WITH OIL; MY CUP OVERFLOWS

When the flock reached the tableland, Precious was dazzled. "It's beautiful. It's wonderful," she gushed as she looked at the level ground, the tender grass, and the sparkling water. She felt peace settle over her like a fine misty rain.

"Come on," Sammy called. "Let's get in line."

But the moment was so magical for Precious that she didn't want to get in a line. "Later," she said blissfully.

"No, you don't understand. You won't be able to enjoy the tableland if you don't get in line," Sammy urged.

Precious looked at him in disbelief. "There is nothing that could keep me from enjoying this magnificent place."

"Trust me, one attack of nose flies and you'll forget all about this magnificence," Sammy warned.

"Nose flies," Precious shrieked. "I've heard they will drive you nuts."

"Yep," Sammy nodded. "I didn't get in line last year and they just about drove me crazy. I started running in circles and beating my head against the rocks. I almost killed myself before my shepherd could get to me."

"Well, hurry, let's get in line," Precious said. By this time, she was so hysterical that she began babbling. "Wait a minute. Do you mean that we have to stand in a line of sheep the whole summer? Will we have to sleep in a line? Oh, my—standing in a line, sleeping in a line, eating in a line, drinking in a line. I don't think I'm going to like this place after all."

Sammy chuckled. "Take a deep breath and calm down Precious. We just have to get in line for our shepherd to pour oil on our heads. He has special oil that will keep us from getting nose flies."

Precious was speechless. "Why do I always make everything so hard?" she finally asked.

"It takes time to learn to trust our shepherd," Sammy said with a smile. "The more you know him, the more you'll trust him. You'll even trust him when you don't understand what he's doing or why he's doing it."

While Sammy and Precious waited for their shepherd to put the oil on their heads, Precious pondered all that Sammy had told her about their shepherd. After a while, she turned to Sammy and said: "Since our shepherd bought me, I have been living as if there was only a drop of his love in my cup. And I think I was afraid that the last drop would be gone any minute. I think I'm beginning to understand that my cup will never be empty. It is always overflowing with his love."

Sammy was flabbergasted. "Precious—you've got it! Our shepherd's love does not depend on who we are, what we do, or where we are. He will always love us. His love never fails."

"Now, if I can just remember it," Precious smiled.

"TALK ABOUT IT."
CHAPTER 9 • PAGE 54

SURELY GOODNESS AND MERCY SHALL FOLLOW ME ALL THE DAYS OF MY LIFE

Precious stamped her hoof disgustedly. "Bertha is so annoying," she said to Sammy. "Whenever I am playing with someone, she wants to play with us. When we divide into teams for a game, she wants to be on my team—and she is so awkward and slow that she makes our team lose. When I'm trying to rest, she wants to talk. She acts as if she's my best friend. And she's so bossy. She really aggravates me."

Sammy didn't say anything.

"Why are you so quiet?" Precious asked. Now she felt annoyed with Sammy.

"I'm trying to decide whether now is a good time to teach you something our shepherd taught me."

"Why wouldn't this be a good time?" Precious snapped.

"Do you think your heart is ready to hear something wonderful, even if it hurts at first?" Sammy asked.

Precious wasn't sure she liked the way this conversation was going, but in her heart she knew that Sammy was her friend. He would do only what was good for her.

"I'm not sure," she answered honestly. "But I probably need to hear whatever you're going to tell me."

Sammy smiled. "OK, here goes. But you'd better not roll your eyes and give me that look."

"What look?"

"The I'm-so-annoyed-with-you look," he teased.

"Do I give that look?" Precious asked rather sheepishly.

"Oh, yeah," Sammy laughed.

"Then I think I need to hear what you have to tell me."

"Well, Precious," Sammy began, "I used to get annoyed with other sheep all the time. And I had no mercy toward the weaker sheep. It irritated me that they took so much of the shepherd's time and that we all had to help them."

Precious was startled. "Sammy, I can't imagine you getting annoyed with anyone," she said. "You're so good and kind."

"But you didn't know me before our shepherd taught me what I'm going to tell you. Here it is, and I hope you'll never forget it: there are no annoying sheep, just annoyed sheep."

Sammy paused and let his words hang in the air so that Precious could think about what he had said.

"Soooo," Precious said slowly, "the problem is not the other sheep. The problem is . . . me?"

"Yep," Sammy agreed.

"You're sure Bertha is not the problem?" Precious asked.

"Think about it, Precious. What is one thing that is true of every sheep in our flock, even Bertha?"

Precious pondered this a bit and then said: "Our good shepherd bought every one of us. We all belong to him. Oh, Sammy, how could I be annoyed with a sheep that our shepherd loves? But I'm confused. Is it right for Bertha to . . . well . . . to be like she is?"

Sammy nodded understandingly. "If Bertha needs to change, our shepherd will change her," he said. "We're supposed to accept and love each other. Of course, we should also help each other."

Precious nodded. "Just like you're helping me," she said. "But Sammy, why are we all so different? It would be easier if we were all alike."

"It would also be very boring," Sammy explained. "And how would we learn to show goodness and mercy if we were all alike? Our shepherd knew what we were like before he bought us. He planned for our flock to be exactly the way it is."

"Oh, Sammy, you're so wise. I'm so bad, and I'm so tired of trying to be good. I don't think I'll ever be good enough to belong to our shepherd."

"You're right about that," Sammy said. "None of us can ever be good enough to belong to our shepherd. But here's the good news. He loves us because we're his. He doesn't love us more when we're good and he doesn't love us less when we're bad. He loves us perfectly all the time. His love is a gift, and it's a gift that we can't earn and we don't deserve. It's called grace."

"I don't think my sheep brain is big enough to hold that," Precious sighed.

"You're right about that, too," Sammy laughed. "But the more you trust him, the more his grace and mercy will overflow from you to others."

"TALK ABOUT IT."
CHAPTER 10 • PAGE 55

AND I SHALL DWELL IN THE HOUSE OF THE LORD FOREVER

Summer is almost over. Soon we'll start our journey back home," Sammy told Precious one glorious morning as they watched the sun rise over the mountains.

"I'm ready," Precious sighed.

"You're not afraid?" Sammy asked.

"No, I've learned to trust our shepherd. He's merciful. He bought me when I was sick and dirty, and he has cared for me so that now I'm strong and healthy. He's good. He always does what is good and right for me. He has forgiven me when I've disobeyed him, comforted me when I've been fearful, and rescued me when I've wandered away. I have finally realized that I'm a precious jewel to him, and that I will dwell in his flock forever."

The two sheep were silent. They watched the grass bow down as the soft breeze floated through the air.

"Actually, I'm excited about going back home," Precious said.

"Really?" Sammy asked. "Why?"

"Because I hope that when our shepherd brings new sheep to our flock, I can help them to know and trust him."

"Ah—very good. That's the way it's supposed to be in our shepherd's flock. One sheep tells another about our wonderful shepherd, so that each generation learns to trust him."

Sammy and Precious listened to the sweet silence again. They both pondered the goodness and mercy of their shepherd. Once again, it was Precious who interrupted the silence.

"Sammy, thank you for showing and telling me about our shepherd. I have seen his goodness and mercy spill out of your heart onto me. You taught me. You've been kind to me. You made me feel that I belonged in this flock. You've been patient with me when I was annoyed with you, and you have forgiven me when I was unkind. You're like our shepherd."

"Really?" Sammy asked in amazement.

"Yes. You taught me something you didn't even realize you were teaching me."

Now Sammy was really baffled. "What are you talking about Precious?"

"You have shown me that the more we know our shepherd, the more we become like him. He is good and merciful, and when we live with him we become good and merciful, too. Being with him changes us from silly sheep to faithful followers."

Rays of sunlight danced on the grass. The two sheep were silent again, too overcome with wonder to say a word. Finally, Precious spoke with confidence and conviction: "I will dwell in our shepherd's flock forever. I know that even if I stray away, he will come after me and bring me home because he loves me and I belong to him. I can't wait to tell others about him."

"TALK ABOUT IT."
CHAPTER 11 • PAGE 56

"TALK ABOUT IT."

CHAPTER ONE

THE LORD IS MY SHEPHERD; I SHALL NOT WANT

The Bible tells us:

Jesus said: "I am the good shepherd. I know my own and my own know me" (John 10:14).

"He calls his own sheep by name" (John 10:3).

"I am the good shepherd. The good shepherd lays down his life for the sheep" (John 10:11).

Something to talk about:

- Why was Sammy a happy sheep?
- What does the name *Samuel* mean?
- What are some things Sammy knew about his shepherd?
- Was the sheep in the other pasture happy?
- What did Sammy do to show kindness to the little sheep?
- Who is our Good Shepherd?

Something to do:

Thank Jesus that He is your Shepherd and that He knows your name.

CHAPTER TWO
HE MAKES ME LIE DOWN IN GREEN PASTURES

The Bible tells us:

We are like sheep. We cannot rest in our hearts if we are afraid, but our Good Shepherd has promised that He will never leave us:

"I will never leave you nor forsake you" (Hebrews 13:5b).

We cannot rest when we are angry with each other. But we can love each other because Jesus first loved us:

Beloved, let us love one another, for love is from God, and whoever loves has been born of God and knows God. . . . We love because he first loved us (1 John 4:7, 19).

We cannot rest if we are not peaceful. It's usually not bugs that bother us. It may be irritations like a younger brother who plays with our toys or an older sister who bosses us. Sometimes we are agitated because we don't get what we want. But Jesus gives us peace:

And he shall stand and shepherd his flock in the strength of the LORD, in the majesty of the name of the LORD his God. And they shall dwell secure . . . And he shall be their peace (Micah 5:4–5a).

We cannot rest when our souls are hungry for love, peace, and joy. Our Good Shepherd has done everything to feed us spiritual food. He is the Bread of Life who satisfies our souls:

"Jesus said to them, 'I am the bread of life; whoever comes to me shall not hunger, and whoever believes in me shall never thirst'" (John 6:35).

We can have rest in our hearts because the Lord is our Shepherd. He will give us everything we need to be happy in Him.

- What four things keep sheep from being able to lie down and rest?
- What are some things that cause you to be afraid? What has Jesus promised?
- What makes you angry with others? What does Jesus give us grace to do?
- What makes you agitated and worried? What does Jesus give us?
- What do our souls hunger for? Who is the Bread of Life?

Something to do:

Ask Jesus for grace to trust Him, to love others, to be peaceful, and to be satisfied with Him.

CHAPTER THREE

HE LEADS ME BESIDE STILL WATERS

The Bible tells us:

> *"Whoever drinks of the water that I will give him will never be thirsty forever. The water that I will give him will become in him a spring of water welling up to eternal life" (John 4:14).*

Of course, Jesus was not talking about water like you drink out of a glass. He was talking about spiritual water. He was talking about Himself.

Something to talk about:

- When is your favorite time of the day?
- What do you like to think about in your quiet times?
- Why did Sammy love the other sheep?

Something to do:

Every morning, ask Jesus to help you to be thirsty for the Water of Life—Him.

Think about the people in your family and your church. What is something you love about each of them?

CHAPTER FOUR

HE RESTORES MY SOUL

The Bible tells us:

We don't roll over on our backs and become helpless like sheep sometimes do, but our souls become cast down. When that happens, we need our Shepherd to restore us.

Sometimes we want everything to be soft and easy, but our Good Shepherd knows that we need some hard times to make us strong and to help us learn to trust Him.

Sometimes our lives become tangled with sin. When we are angry, disobedient, disrespectful, or selfish, our souls become cast down. But if we ask our Good Shepherd to forgive us, He cleanses us from sin and restores us.

If we confess our sins, he is faithful and just to forgive us our sins and to cleanse us from all unrighteousness (1 John 1:9).

Something to talk about:

- What does it mean for a sheep to be cast down?
- How does a sheep get into a cast position?
- Can a sheep restore himself to a right position?
- What causes our souls to be cast down?
- Who restores us?

Something to do:

Is there anything hard in your life right now? Ask Jesus to use it to help you trust Him more.

Is there some sin in your heart? Ask Jesus to give you grace to repent. Ask Him to cleanse you from that sin.

CHAPTER FIVE
HE LEADS ME IN PATHS OF RIGHTEOUSNESS FOR HIS NAME'S SAKE

The Bible tells us:

But now thus says the LORD, he who created you . . .
"Fear not, for I have redeemed you; I have called you by name, you are mine.
When you pass through the waters, I will be with you. . . .
For I am the LORD your God, the Holy One of Israel, your Savior. . . .
You are precious in my eyes, and honored, and I love you"
(Isaiah 43:1–4a).

Something to talk about:

• What did My Friend decide to do?
• What happened to her?
• What was the only way she could become part of the good shepherd's flock?
• What did he name her?

Something to do:

Read 1 Peter 1:18–19:
"You were not redeemed with corruptible things, like silver or gold . . . but with the precious blood of Christ, as of a lamb without blemish and without spot" (NKJV).

Thank Jesus that He redeemed you with His own blood. Thank Him that you are precious to Him.

EVEN THOUGH I WALK THROUGH THE VALLEY OF THE SHADOW OF DEATH, I WILL FEAR NO EVIL, FOR YOU ARE WITH ME

The Bible tells us:

"The sheep hear his voice, and he calls his own sheep by name and leads them out. . . . He goes before them, and the sheep follow him, for they know his voice" (John 10:3b–4).

The Lord GOD comes with might. . . . He will tend his flock like a shepherd; he will gather the lambs in his arms; he will carry them in his bosom . . . (Isaiah 40:10–11a).

Something to talk about:

- What was the first thing Precious thought about in the morning and the last thing she thought about at night?
- What is the first thing you think about in the morning and the last thing you think about at night?
- How did Sammy encourage Precious when she was afraid to go to the high places?
- What happened when Precious became tired and afraid that she would get lost?
- Do you ever feel afraid and alone? What should you remember?

Something to do:

Read Isaiah 40:10–11a again. Thank Jesus that He carries you in His bosom, close to His heart.

Pray that you will encourage your friends like Sammy encouraged Precious.

CHAPTER SEVEN

YOUR ROD AND YOUR STAFF, THEY COMFORT ME

The Bible tells us:

> *"For thus says the Lord GOD: Behold, I, I myself will search for my sheep and will seek them out. As a shepherd seeks out his flock when he is among his sheep that have been scattered, so will I seek out my sheep, and I will rescue them"* (Ezekiel 34:11–12a).

The Bible is our Good Shepherd's rod. When we store it in our hearts, the Bible keeps us from wandering away from God:

> *I have stored up your word in my heart, that I might not sin against you* (Psalm 119:11).

The Holy Spirit is like the shepherd's staff. The Holy Spirit teaches us and pulls us to God and to one another. He helps us to love God and other people:

> *"But the Helper, the Holy Spirit, whom the Father will send in my name, he will teach you all things and bring to your remembrance all that I have said to you"* (John 14:26).

The Bible and the Holy Spirit are the equipment God has given to the Good Shepherd. He uses them to equip us to trust and obey Him. That should comfort us.

Something to talk about:

- When Precious was alarmed, what did Sammy tell her to do?
- Why did the shepherd's rod and staff comfort Sammy?
- What is our Good Shepherd's rod?
- What is His staff?
- What are some ways we become careless and stray away from Jesus?
- How was Sammy a good friend to Precious?

Read Hebrews 13:20-21:

"Now may the God of peace who brought again from the dead our Lord Jesus, the great shepherd of the sheep, by the blood of the eternal covenant, equip you with everything good that you may do his will, working in us that which is pleasing in his sight, through Jesus Christ, to whom be glory forever and ever. Amen.

Thank God that Jesus, our Great Shepherd, equips us with everything we need to do His will.

CHAPTER EIGHT

YOU PREPARE A TABLE BEFORE ME IN
THE PRESENCE OF MY ENEMIES

The Bible tells us:

"Let not your hearts be troubled. Believe in God; believe also in me. In my Father's house are many rooms. If it were not so, would I have told you that I go to prepare a place for you? And if I go and prepare a place for you, I will come again and will take you to myself, that where I am you may be also" (John 14:1–3).

Jesus went before us and prepared the way. He defeated our enemy Satan. He invites us to His table. Each time our church celebrates the Lord's Supper, we remember that He conquered our enemy by dying on the cross for our sins, that He has gone to prepare a home for us in heaven, and that one day He will take us to that heavenly tableland where He will feed us at His table.

Something to talk about:

• Why was Sammy patient with Precious?
• Why did he love to answer her questions?
• What is a tableland?
• What does a good shepherd do to prepare the tableland?
• What place has Jesus prepared for us?
• When your church observes the Lord's Supper, what should you remember?

Something to do:

Think about the people who answer your questions about our Good Shepherd. Thank them for teaching you about Jesus.

CHAPTER NINE

You Anoint My Head With Oil; My Cup Overflows

The Bible tells us:

> *"'And in the last days it shall be,' God declares, 'that I will pour out my Spirit on all flesh'" (Acts 2:17a).*

When Jesus rose from the dead and ascended to heaven, He poured out His Holy Spirit on His people (Acts 2:32–33). The Holy Spirit teaches and guides us. He comforts us. He reminds us of God's love. And He gives us grace so that irritations and problems don't drive us nuts.

> *Thus says the LORD: . . . "I have loved you with an everlasting love; therefore I have continued my faithfulness to you" (Jeremiah 31:2–3).*

We can never be good enough to earn God's love. He loves us because we are His. He loves us perfectly. His love will never end.

Something to talk about:

- What did the shepherd do to protect the sheep from flies?
- What did Precious finally realize about her shepherd's love?
- What does God pour into our hearts?
- Can we be good enough to earn God's love?
- How long will our Shepherd love us?

Something to do:

Read John 3:16:

> *"For God so loved the world, that he gave his only Son, that whoever believes in him should not perish but have eternal life."*

Thank God for loving you so much that He sent Jesus to be your Good Shepherd and to give His life for you.

CHAPTER TEN

SURELY GOODNESS AND MERCY SHALL FOLLOW ME ALL THE DAYS OF MY LIFE

The Bible tells us:

Therefore welcome one another as Christ has welcomed you, for the glory of God (Romans 15:7).

God accepts us into His family because Jesus took our place and died for our sins. We are not accepted because of anything we ever did or ever will do. We are to accept others because God accepts us. When we do this, we give praise to God and we show others what He is like.

Something to talk about:

- When Precious was annoyed, what did Sammy teach her?
- What does it mean to say, "There are no annoying sheep, just annoyed sheep"?
- Can we be good enough to earn our way into God's family?
- Who loved us so much that He made the way for us to be in God's family?
- Why should we accept others?

Something to do:

When you are annoyed with someone, ask Jesus to forgive you for being annoyed. Then ask Him to give you grace to accept and love that person and to show him or her God's goodness and grace.

CHAPTER ELEVEN

AND I SHALL DWELL IN THE HOUSE OF THE LORD FOREVER

The Bible tells us:

> *And we all, with unveiled face, beholding the glory of the Lord, are being transformed into the same image from one degree of glory to another. For this comes from the Lord who is the Spirit (2 Corinthians 3:18).*

Something to talk about:

- Why was Precious ready to go back home?
- What did Sammy teach Precious that he didn't realize he was teaching her?
- What does being with Jesus change us from?
- If we trust Jesus to save us from our sin, where will we live for all eternity?

Something to do:

Thank Jesus that He is your Good Shepherd.

Ask Jesus to change you so that you become more and more like Him.

Memorize Psalm 23 and remember it all the days of your life.

Tell others about your Good Shepherd.

ABOUT THE AUTHOR

Susan Hunt is a consultant for the Presbyterian Church in America's Women in the Church ministry, which she formerly directed. She holds a degree in Christian education from Columbia Theological Seminary and has written Sunday school curricula for Great Commission Publications. She is a popular speaker at conferences in the United States and abroad. Her numerous published books include *Women's Ministry in the Local Church* (co-authored with Dr. J. Ligon Duncan III) and *Heirs of the Covenant*, plus such children's titles as *My ABC Bible Verses* and *Big Truths for Little Kids* (co-authored with her son Richie Hunt). Susan and her husband, Gene, a retired pastor, make their home in Marietta, Georgia. They have three adult children and twelve grandchildren.

ABOUT THE ILLUSTRATOR

Cory Godbey is an illustrator and author with Portland Studios in Greenville, South Carolina. As he tells it, Cory discovered his love for drawing in math class and soon began drawing pictures for elementary school textbooks. He eventually went to college to study old drawings by well-known artists, and he says he still looks at these old drawings when he runs out of ideas. He enjoys lively accordion music, pasta, and rain at night. He and his wife, Erin Elizabeth, live in South Carolina with their cats Harrel Whittington and James.